Ruby the Reindeer

By Sophia Rico and Martin Rico

Written with love for Penelope

It was Christmas Eve morning at the North Pole. The elves were happily making toys, all except one. Holly was a small elf with big dreams. She wished that someday she could be the first girl Chief Elf.

Just yesterday, she had shared her dream with the other elves, but they just laughed at her. Even Pipsqueak laughed, the tiniest elf of all. Holly finished wrapping a present and placed it in Santa's sack of toys.

Later that morning, the elves were almost finished loading up Santa's sleigh, when all of a sudden Jack Frost appeared out of nowhere. All the elves gasped and poor little Pipsqueak fainted.

Jack Frost announced, "This year, I'm going to make the biggest blizzard the world has ever seen. This year, Christmas won't come!"

Holly knelt down and helped Pipsqueak up. She looked at Jack Frost, found her courage, and said, "We have Santa and the best reindeer in the world. They can get through any old blizzard. You'll never stop Christmas, Jack Frost!"

"Well then I'll take the reindeer away where you will never find them!" Jack Frost said, and with a poof, he and all the reindeer disappeared. Pipsqueak fainted again.

Santa told the elves, "Now, don't you worry. Everything will be fine. We'll get the reindeer back."

"But how?" asked Chief Elf Kringle-Whiner. "Jack Frost could have taken them anywhere! We're doomed!"

"We are most certainly not doomed," Santa said. "We won't let Jack Frost stop Christmas. I'll send the detective elves to find him. They will find his hideout in no time."

The sky darkened. A great northerly wind blew so hard it howled. Snow and ice fell in sheets, and a deep fog set in. It was the greatest snow storm the world had ever seen, just as Jack Frost promised.

Holly and the elves kept loading the sleigh, but none of them could stop worrying. That afternoon, Santa called the elves together and announced, "None of our detective elves have been able to find Jack Frost. The storm is so strong, they can't see a thing, so I've decided to go after him myself."

    "But wait!" cried Chief Elf Kringle-Whiner. "Will you be back in time for Christmas? We only have a few hours before you have to leave. If you're not back, what will we do!? I told you we were doomed!"

    "Everything will be fine. Don't worry," Santa said. "I'll be back with plenty of time to spare," and with a touch of his nose, Santa disappeared with a poof.

Holly and the other elves finished loading the sleigh. The hours passed slowly. The Christmas Eve party was canceled. The elves just stood around the sleigh, hoping Santa and the reindeer would poof back and jump into action.

Finally, at five minutes until Christmas, Mrs. Claus walked up to the sleigh. "Santa should be here any minute. He has to leave soon or he won't have enough time to deliver all the presents," she said.

The big clock in the workshop started to chime. It was officially Christmas Day, but Santa still wasn't in sight. Fifteen minutes passed with no Santa. Then thirty. Then forty-five, and still no Santa. The elves were absolutely frantic when Mrs. Claus announced, "I'm afraid to say that Christmas may be canceled this year."

All the elves gasped and three small elves burst into tears. Pipsqueak almost had a heart attack and was carried off on a stretcher by two doctor-elves.

Holly was so sad she couldn't bear to stay in the workshop, so she put on her heavy jacket and went on a little walk. Out of the corner of her eye, she saw a faint glow far off in the woods.

"What could that be?" she wondered aloud.

She knew she should stay with Mrs. Claus and the elves, but her curiosity got the best of her. She followed the glow until she found herself in an opening in the woods that was protected from the storm by a mountain. Eight reindeer were swooping up and down in the air, swerving, diving, and chasing each other.

One reindeer stood by a tree watching them. Holly walked up to her. "Hi. I'm Holly. What's your name?"

"They call me Ruby."

"What are you reindeer doing over here? Why weren't you with the others back in the workshop?"

"Girl reindeer aren't allowed in there. Some kind of old rule, but that's OK. We have lots of fun over here playing flying freeze tag, flying frisbee golf, all kinds of games."

"How come you're not playing?"

"I'm way too fast. It wouldn't be fair, but they let me have a turn once in a while."

And just then one of the reindeer called out from the sky, "OK Ruby, you can have a turn now. You're it!"

Ruby blasted off so fast, she left a ruby-red glow in her wake, like a rocket launching toward the stars. All the reindeer were tagged and frozen within five seconds.

"I win again!" cried Ruby. "Wo-hoo!"

Seeing the reindeer and how fast Ruby was made Holly jump for joy. "Ruby, come back quick. I have to tell you something."

Holly explained about Jack Frost and the missing reindeer and asked if they could fill in. When all the reindeer said they were more than happy to help, they sprinted back to Santa's workshop where they found Mrs. Claus sitting by the fire looking miserable. After a little convincing, Mrs. Claus said, "Well it's the only plan we've got, so let's go and let's go fast!"

They raced to the sleigh. The elves rejoiced and quickly started putting harnesses on the reindeer, but when they explained their plan to Chief Elf Kringle-Whiner, he folded his arms and shook his head. "No, no, no! That is not allowed. A girl reindeer has never flown the sleigh. These little girls will never even get the sleigh off the ground, and as Chief Elf, it is my job to ride with Santa and distribute presents. I ride with Santa only. No substitutes."

"But it's our only chance to save Christmas," Holly said.

"Yes, but think of everything that could go wrong. I won't allow it!"

"We have to try."

"I said no, and if you do not obey the rules, you will be kicked out of the North Pole!"

Holly and all the elves hung their heads low and said nothing else.
Ruby folded her arms and kicked a rock. "This stinks!"

"Now everyone go back to your homes. I'm afraid Christmas really is canceled," Chief Elf Kringle-Whiner said.

The elves fell silent and started heading home, but Holly stayed put. She thought about all the boys and girls who were counting on her and found her courage again. "No," she said. "We can't just give up. We have the reindeer. We have Mrs. Claus who can drive the sleigh. We can do it!"

"The rules are the rules and one more word from you and you'll be kicked out of the North Pole tonight."

Holly was about to say something when Mrs. Claus put her hand on her shoulder. "That's enough for now, Holly."

Mrs. Claus walked up to the Chief Elf. "Oh Kringle-Whiner, you worry too much," she said, and with a tap of her nose, he poofed up to the top of the giant Christmas tree.

"Get me down from here this instant! This is an outrage!" he cried out, shaking his fist to the air.

Mrs. Claus looked at the elves. "When the rules are wrong, they have to change." The elves and reindeer jumped up and down, and hooted and whistled their approval.

"Elves, get these reindeer harnessed," Mrs. Claus said. "Ruby, to the head of my sleigh."

Ruby stood at attention and saluted. "Sure thing, boss."

When all the reindeer were ready, Mrs. Claus turned to Holly, gave her a big, warm smile, and said, "Holly, we could never have done this without you. Will you please be my Chief Elf tonight?"

"What, me? Deliver presents?"

"Yes, you Holly. We still have a lot to do to save Christmas, and I need someone brave enough to believe we can succeed to help."

"Yes! Yes, of course I'll do it!" she exclaimed, then jumped for joy and hopped into the sleigh.

The elves opened the doors, letting in the howling wind and snow.
"But wait. How will we get through the storm?" Holly asked.
"You're right. We still can't see a thing."

Ruby pulled herself out of her harness and flew to them. "I've got an idea," she said, then zoomed over to the giant Christmas tree, flying round and round it at lightning speed.

"Good heavens!" cried Kringle-Whiner, who was still stuck at the top.

Then Ruby flew all over the workshop and back so fast all you could see was a red streak zooming around the sleigh. When she was done, every Christmas light in the workshop was wrapped around the sleigh and the reindeer too, including Ruby, who was back in her harness. The sleigh now shined so bright, it was almost as dazzling as the star of Bethlehem.

"That's perfect!" cried out Mrs. Claus. "We're ready!"
Then she called out:
"Now, Debbie! Now, Dora! Now Piper and Jasmin!
On, Chloe! On, Carmen! On Duchess and Kaitlyn!
Ruby, to the top of the storm! To the top of the sky!
One, two, here we go!"

The sleigh flew off the ground and all the elves cheered. "Christmas is saved!"
Pipsqueak was crying tears of joy. "You're my hero, Holly!" he yelled out. "And
you too, Ruby! You're the greatest reindeer of all!"

They flew over the snow clouds and Mrs. Claus called out, "Merry Christmas to all, and to all a good night!"

Ruby knew they were running late, so she turned and spoke to the other reindeer, "Top speed girls. Let's show them what we've got!" The reindeers' legs chugged and chugged like a choo-choo train, and after a few seconds the sleigh took off at incredible speed. All that could be seen from Santa's workshop was a ruby-red streak racing through the sky.

The next morning when the sleigh landed in front of the workshop, all the elves were cheering. Santa was too, and all the reindeer, who had been rescued just a few hours before.

Santa was so impressed and grateful that Holly had helped save Christmas, he declared her the first girl Chief Elf and proclaimed that next year, the sleigh would be pulled by all of the boy and girl reindeer together, with Ruby at the head of the sleigh.